RAINBOW magic

SPECIAL EDITION

EMMA
THE EASTER FAIRY

By Daisy Meadows
Illustrated by Georgie Ripper

Silver Dolphin

Silver Dolphin Books
An imprint of Printers Row Publishing Group
A division of Readerlink Distribution Services, LLC
9717 Pacific Heights Blvd, San Diego, CA 92121
www.silverdolphinbooks.com

Printers Row Publishing Group is a division of
Readerlink Distribution Services, LLC.
Silver Dolphin Books is a registered trademark of
Readerlink Distribution Services, LLC.

All notations of errors or omissions should be addressed to Silver Dolphin Books,
Editorial Department, at the above address. All other correspondence (author
inquiries, permissions) concerning the content of this book should be addressed to:
Hachette Children's Group
Carmelite House
50 Victoria Embankment
London
EC4Y 0DZ

ISBN: 978-1-6672-0239-6
Manufactured, printed, and assembled in Guangzhou, China.
First printing, September 2023. GD/09/23
27 26 25 24 23   1 2 3 4 5

Table of Contents

The
Fairyland
Palace

Emma's
Toadstool
Cottage

Pet
Store

Wetherbury
Village

Park

Strawberry
Farm

The Easter Bunny's Cottage

Jack Frost's Ice Castle

Mr. Hopper's Market

Kirsty's House

Daffodil Field

EASTER CANDY TASTES SO SWEET,
COLORED EGGS ARE A PRETTY TREAT.
AND CHILDREN SMILE ON EASTER DAY
WHEN THE EASTER BUNNY COMES THEIR WAY.

BUT I'LL MAKE CHOCOLATE MELT AWAY.
THERE WON'T BE COLORED EGGS TODAY.
AND NOBODY WILL THINK IT'S FUNNY,
WHEN I KIDNAP THE EASTER BUNNY!

Find the hidden letters in the chicks
throughout the book. Unscramble all
nine letters to spell out a special Easter
treat! See page 164 for the answer.

THE SWEET TREAT DISASTER

TABLE OF CONTENTS

A MELTED MESS!

"We're finally here!" Rachel Walker cried as her dad pulled the car to a stop in the driveway.

Rachel's best friend, Kirsty Tate, ran across the lawn to say hello.

"We have so many fun things planned," Kirsty said. "We're going to dye eggs for the big Easter egg hunt, and go to Strawberry Farm, and—"

"First we have to unpack," Mrs. Walker

said as Rachel got out of the car. "Rachel, why don't you and Kirsty grab the cooler?"

Rachel and Kirsty each took a handle of the blue cooler and carried it toward Kirsty's house.

"I'm so glad your Aunt Sally lives near Wetherbury," Kirsty said.

"Me, too," agreed Rachel. "We'll have Easter dinner with Aunt Sally, but first we get to spend two whole days with you!" The two girls had met on vacation at Rainspell Island. They were always excited to have a chance to visit each other.

They carried the cooler up the steps to Kirsty's front door.

"This is heavy!" Kirsty remarked. "What's in it?"

Rachel grinned. "It's a special surprise."

When they entered the kitchen, Rachel's parents were talking with Mr. and Mrs. Tate.

"Good to see you, Rachel," said Kirsty's mom.

"What are you carrying in that cooler?"

"Can I tell them, Mom?" Rachel asked.

Mrs. Walker nodded, smiling.

"Mom and I made special Easter chocolates," Rachel said. "There are bunnies, flowers, chicks, and even chocolate eggs. We wrapped them in sparkly paper, too! They look so pretty."

Rachel opened the lid to show them.

"Oh, no!" She gasped.

"What's wrong?" Kirsty asked.

Inside the cooler, the chocolates had melted into one big, gooey mess! The sparkly wrappers had slipped off and fallen into the sticky chocolate.

"They're all ruined!" Rachel cried.

Mrs. Walker looked over Rachel's shoulder and frowned. "That's odd," she said. She felt the inside of the lid. "We filled the cooler with plenty of ice packs.

It still feels chilly inside. The chocolates shouldn't have melted."

Rachel tried not to look too sad, but she couldn't help it.

"But they did. Now there's no chocolate for Easter."

"Don't forget about the Easter Bunny," Mrs. Tate reminded her. "I'm sure he'll bring you lots of chocolate in your Easter basket."

"He always does," Kirsty said, trying to cheer up her friend.

"I'd better clean this up," said Rachel's mom. "Why don't you girls go outside for a while? It's a beautiful day."

The girls headed outside and sat on Kirsty's front porch. Pretty pink and yellow tulips bloomed in the flowerbed there.

13

"It's strange that the chocolate melted, even though the cooler was chilly," Kirsty remarked.

Rachel nodded. "I was thinking the same thing," she said. She lowered her voice. "Do you think Jack Frost is behind it somehow?"

The girls had a special secret. They were friends with the fairies! Because of their special friendship, they knew Jack Frost and his goblins were always causing trouble in Fairyland. Sometimes they played their tricks in the human world, too.

"Maybe," Kirsty replied. "But it's hard to believe there could be goblins around on a nice sunny day like today."

"A beautiful day won't keep the goblins away!" a musical voice cried just then.

One of the pink tulips began to wiggle.

14

The petals opened up, and a tiny fairy
flew out! The air shimmered around her
as she flew toward the girls.

"You must be Rachel and Kirsty," said
the fairy, twirling in the air. "I'm Emma
the Easter Fairy!"

15

Emma wore a pastel yellow dress with a pretty pink sash around the waist. She had polka-dotted rain boots on her feet, and her bouncy curls were held back with a flowery headband.

"It's nice to meet you," Rachel said.

"Hi, Emma," said Kirsty. "Happy Easter!"

"I'm afraid there might not be a happy Easter this year," Emma said, perching on Kirsty's shoulder and looking glum. "The Easter Bunny is missing!"

EMMA'S STORY

"Missing!" Rachel exclaimed. "Did Jack Frost kidnap him?"

"I'll bet he did," Kirsty said. "Jack Frost has done things like that before. Remember the time he stole Santa's sleigh?"

"That's exactly what I thought," Emma said. "But he's getting even trickier! Let me show you."

19

Emma waved her wand, and in a burst of sparkles, two Easter eggs appeared in midair. Rachel and Kirsty each took one. Each eggshell was painted with pretty flowers.

"Look through the pointy end," Emma told them.

Each of the eggs had a small window on one end. Both girls looked through the windows.

"It's Fairyland!" Rachel exclaimed.

"That's right," Emma said. "And that's my cottage."

Thanks to Emma's fairy magic, they could see inside Emma's red-and-white toadstool cottage. Emma was happily painting Easter eggs with a paintbrush. There was a white chicken perched on the chair behind her, watching.

"It's my job to add the extra sparkle to Easter," Emma explained. "Every year, my pet chicken, Fluffy, lays three magical eggs. On the first egg, I paint a picture of a chocolate bunny. That egg helps to make Easter chocolate extra yummy."

"Mmm," said Kirsty, licking her lips. "I love Easter candy."

"On the second egg, I paint a picture of a colorful Easter egg," Emma told them. "That egg helps make all of the dyed Easter eggs bright and beautiful."

"So that's why Easter eggs always look so pretty!" Rachel said.

Emma nodded, looking proud. "On the third egg, I paint an Easter basket," the fairy went on. "That's the most important egg of all! It gives the Easter Bunny the extra magical push he needs to deliver all of the Easter baskets in just one night."

The girls held the eggs to their eyes again and watched the story unfold. They saw Emma put the finishing touches on her final painted egg. Then she smiled, gave Fluffy a pat on the head, and flew off.

"I wanted to tell the Easter Bunny that I had finished the eggs," Emma said. "But when I got to his cottage, he wasn't there! I looked all over Fairyland, but I couldn't find him."

In the pictures, the girls saw Emma flying around Fairyland. Finally, she went to the castle to find Queen Titania and King Oberon.

"I told them that the Easter Bunny was missing," Emma explained. "Right away, they suspected Jack Frost. Last year, Jack tried to use a spell to make all of the Easter eggs rotten. The Easter Bunny stopped him, and Jack Frost has been angry ever since."

"That proves it!" Kirsty said, looking defiant. "Jack Frost *must* have kidnapped the Easter Bunny!"

"Watch and see," Emma said.

In the pictures, Emma followed the king and queen as they rushed to Jack Frost's Ice Castle. Jack Frost sat on his icy throne, grinning.

"He told us he had no idea where the Easter Bunny was," Emma said. "He invited the king and queen to search the castle. But the Easter Bunny was nowhere to be found."

"So was Jack Frost telling the truth?" Rachel asked.

"It looked that way," Emma said. "But then I suddenly remembered the three magic eggs in my cottage. I had a bad feeling about them, so I flew back home as quickly as I could."

The picture inside the eggs changed again. Emma flew toward her toadstool cottage. The girls could see Jack Frost's goblins heading toward her house too! Emma waved her wand, and silver glitter floated through the air.

25

THE SWEET TREAT DISASTER

The magic glitter trickled inside the cottage and surrounded the three magic eggs. The eggs disappeared just as the goblins burst through the door. They were safe!

"I sent the eggs here to Wetherbury," Emma said. "I don't know where they

ended up, but they should be safe from
the goblins."

"But not for long," Rachel pointed out.
"We need to find them first."

"Not only that," Kirsty added, "but we
have to find the Easter Bunny, too!"

GOBLINS IN THE MARKET

"Emma, is that why our Easter chocolates melted?" Rachel asked. "Because the magic eggs are missing?"

Emma nodded, and her curls bounced against her shoulders. "Yes. And that's not all. The Easter candy won't taste good. The Easter eggs will go bad. And worst of all, the Easter Bunny won't be able to visit girls and boys on Easter!"

"That sounds terrible!" Kirsty said.

"It would be, but there's still hope,"
Emma said with a smile. "Especially now
that I have you two girls to help me."

Rachel jumped up. "You said the eggs
are somewhere here in Wetherbury. We
should start looking right away!"

"Wetherbury is a big place," Kirsty
reminded her. "It will be hard to find
three small eggs."

Rachel was thoughtful. "Maybe we
should start looking in places where you'd

normally find eggs."

"Like the market!" Kirsty chimed in.

Just then, the girls heard footsteps coming toward the front door.

"Emma, hide!" Rachel said in a loud whisper.

Poof! Emma vanished, leaving a trail of fairy dust shimmering in the air behind her.

And just in time! A moment later, Mrs. Tate and Mrs. Walker stepped onto the porch.

"How are you girls doing?" Mrs. Tate asked.

"Fine, Mom," Kirsty said. "We were thinking about going on a walk. Do you need anything from the market?"

"As a matter of fact, I do," her mom replied.

"I bought some eggs to dye tonight. But they seem to have gone bad already. It's very strange! Mr. Hopper always sells nice, fresh eggs."

"Maybe they were a bad batch," Mrs. Walker suggested.

Rachel and Kirsty looked at each other. They knew that Emma's missing magic egg was the real reason the eggs went bad.

"We'll get some more," Kirsty offered.

Mrs. Tate gave Kirsty money for the eggs, and the girls set off to the town center on foot.

"Wetherbury is very nice," Emma said, suddenly fluttering in the air next to them. "All the pretty flowers remind me of Fairyland."

"Thank you," Kirsty said. "Fairyland is beautiful, too."

32

"But there still isn't any sign of the Easter Bunny there," Emma said. "I hope we can find him soon!"

As they turned the corner, they walked past the pet store. The sign on the door said CLOSED FOR EASTER.

Emma suddenly shivered.

"Emma, are you cold?" Rachel asked, concerned.

"No, this is a different kind of shiver," Emma replied. "Fairies can sense when magic is near. It makes us feel tickly all over." She looked around. "I don't see any other fairies here, do you?"

E

Rachel and Kirsty looked everywhere, but they couldn't see any other fairies.

"No," Rachel said. "And that reminds me—you should hide, before someone sees you!"

"Oh!" Emma said, fluttering around. She settled inside the pocket of Rachel's pink dress. "Is this all right?"

"Just keep your head down," Kirsty whispered.

Only she and Rachel knew about the fairies and their magic, and they had promised to keep them a secret.

A few minutes later, they finally arrived at Mr. Hopper's Market. They opened the door, and a blast of cool air hit them.

"*Now* I'm shivering because I'm cold!" Emma called up from her hiding place.

Right next to the front door was an Easter display. A big stuffed Easter Bunny sat on a mound of fake grass. He held a basket of colorful plastic eggs. A sign on the display read GET YOUR EASTER TREATS HERE!

A long line of people waited at the cash register. They were all holding bags of candy, and they didn't look very happy.

Behind the counter, Mr. Hopper looked awfully worried. Two boys in baseball caps were arguing over by the candy aisle.

"*I* want the green jelly beans!" one boy yelled.

"No, *I* want the green jelly beans!" shouted the other.

Kirsty spotted her friend Andy waiting in the line.

"Andy, why is it so crowded in here?" she asked him.

"Something's wrong with Mr. Hopper's candy," Andy replied. "All the chocolate has melted, even though it's freezing in here. And most of it just doesn't taste right." He held out an open bag of jelly beans. "These taste terrible! You should try one."

Rachel and Kirsty looked at each other.

Eating gross jelly beans didn't sound like fun, but they had to see for themselves.

Kirsty carefully picked out a white jelly bean from the bag. Rachel picked a blue one.

Kirsty popped the jelly bean into her mouth. Then she stuck out her tongue. "This tastes like onions!" she cried.

Rachel made a face. "Mine tastes like blue cheese. *Yuck!*"

37

"Mom wants me to get my money back," Andy said.

Kirsty sighed. "Poor Mr. Hopper!"

Rachel tapped her on the shoulder. "Kirsty, we should go get those eggs for your mom." She lowered her voice so only Kirsty could hear. "Maybe we'll find a magic egg there, too."

They waved good-bye to Andy and walked over to the dairy section, where it was quieter.

Emma popped her head out of Kirsty's pocket. "We have to find the magic egg that makes Easter candy taste delicious— and fast!" she said anxiously.

"Let's start looking through these egg cartons," Rachel suggested.

But before they could, some loud shouts came from the candy aisle. The two

fighting boys were now wrestling over the
bag of green jelly beans. They rolled right
by the girls.

"Give it to me!" one boy cried.

"Never!" replied the other.

The girls jumped back to get out of their
way. Then Rachel noticed something. Both
boys wore baseball caps and jeans. But they
didn't have any shoes on their feet . . . their
green feet.

"Kirsty, those aren't boys at all!" she
whispered. "They're goblins!"

THE JELLY BEAN TRAIL

The girls hurried to the cereal aisle, where the goblins couldn't see them.

"I should have known!" Kirsty said. "Only goblins would fight over green jelly beans."

"They're here for the same reason we are," Emma piped up. "To find the missing magic eggs!"

"Then we have to find them first," Rachel said.

41

Kirsty nodded. "And we have to get those goblins out of here before someone sees them."

The girls heard more shouting from the dairy aisle. They peeked around a shelf and saw three more goblins in disguise, opening up all of the egg cartons! Eggs spilled and cracked on the floor as the goblins carelessly pawed through them.

"Oh, no! What if one of the magic eggs is in there?" Kirsty asked.

Rachel looked thoughtful. She had an idea! "We know that goblins like green jelly beans. Emma, can you use your magic to make some?"

Emma flew out of Rachel's pocket. "Of course! I'm the Easter Fairy. Jelly beans are my speciality!"

"Perfect," Rachel said. "If you make a long trail of green jelly beans from the goblins to the front door, the goblins will follow them outside."

"That's a great idea!" Kirsty agreed. "Just make sure no one sees you, Emma."

Luckily, the customers in the store were too upset about their melted chocolate to notice the goblins. Careful to stay out of sight, Emma flew into the dairy aisle and waved her wand. Green sparkles shot from it. When the sparkles hit the floor, they turned into green jelly beans! Emma made a trail of green jelly beans all the way down the aisle. It didn't take long for the goblins to notice.

"Look—green jelly beans!" one of them cried out.

The two wrestling goblins stopped fighting immediately. The other goblins dropped their egg cartons. All five of them started to race after the jelly beans.

"It's working!" Kirsty cheered quietly.

Emma made a magical trail of jelly beans that led all the way to the front door. The goblins followed the trail, scooping up the jelly beans as they appeared. They shoved and pushed each other to get to them.

Rachel and Kirsty watched the goblins from a safe distance. Once the goblins were outside, the girls would be able to look for the missing magic eggs.

But the goblins stopped before they went through the front door of the market.

"What's happening?" Rachel wondered.

45

THE SWEET TREAT DISASTER

One of the goblins had spotted Mr. Hopper's Easter display. "I think I see something," he said, squinting.

The goblin stuck his hand inside the basket of plastic eggs. Then he pulled out an egg that was glittering with fairy magic. The egg was white, with a picture of a chocolate bunny painted on it.

"I've found one of the missing eggs!" the goblin howled. "Wait until Jack Frost sees this!"

With that, the goblins cheered and raced through the door.

Rachel and Kirsty dashed to catch up to them. "We can't let them get away!" Kirsty cried.

HELP FROM THE SKY

The girls found Emma hovering outside the market door.

"Oh, no!" she said. "My jelly bean trail led those goblins right to the magic egg. What bad luck!"

"They're heading for the park," Kirsty said, pointing. "We can catch up if we hurry."

49

The girls ran fast and almost caught up with the goblins. But the goblins kept going! They ran right into the woods at the edge of the park.

"We might lose them in the trees," Rachel said, worried.

"But we won't," Emma said. "Hold still!"

Emma waved her wand and fairy dust sprinkled out and swirled around the girls. The whirling cloud of glittering dust swept them off of their feet. The girls could feel themselves getting smaller, but they weren't afraid. This had happened to them before.

"We're turning into fairies!" Kirsty cried happily.

"Now we can all fly around the trees and catch up to the goblins," Emma told them.

Rachel took off. "Let's go!"

Rachel was the first to reach the goblin carrying the magic egg. She swooped down and tried to grab it, but the goblin spotted her.

"Hey, it's a fairy!" The goblin scowled. "Hands off my egg!"

He tossed the egg to another goblin. Kirsty flew as fast as she could, hoping to scoop the egg out of the air. But the other goblin jumped up and grabbed it.

"Ha, ha! You can't get it!" the goblin taunted, holding up the egg.

THE SWEET TREAT DISASTER

Emma flew down and tried to take the egg from him. But one of his goblin friends warned him. "Behind you!"

The goblin turned and saw Emma just in time. He threw the egg to another one of his friends.

"This is a fun game!" the goblin said with a nasty smile. "Keep away from the fairies!"

Kirsty flew up to Rachel. "They're too fast!"

At that moment, Emma began to sing a song. It didn't have any words. But it sounded pretty, almost like a bird singing.

Rachel and Kirsty looked at each other. Why was Emma singing at a time like this?

Caw! Caw! Caw!

Five beautiful birds swooped down from the trees, drawn by Emma's song. She had called them to help!

"Friends, please help us get the magic egg back from these goblins!" Emma called out.

The birds dove at the goblin holding the egg.

They pecked at his head with their black beaks. Startled, the goblin dropped the magic egg. One of the birds broke free and grabbed the egg in its claws before it reached the ground.

"Get those birds!" the goblin cried.

But the birds dove at the other goblins. The goblins were so scared that they forgot all about the magic egg! Instead, they shrieked and ran away.

Giggling, Emma sprinkled fairy dust on Rachel and Kirsty again, and they turned back to human-size. One of the birds flew up and gently dropped the egg in Rachel's palm.

"Thank you so much, friends!" Emma told the birds.

The birds flew in a circle around the girls and Emma, tweeting happily. Then they soared off into the trees.

"We did it!" the girls cheered.

"Yes, we did," Emma said happily. "And now I need to get this magic egg back to Fairyland. I'll give it to the king and queen so they can keep it safe."

Emma waved her wand and sprinkled fairy dust over the egg, shrinking it back to fairy-size. Then Emma took the egg from Rachel.

"Good-bye, girls—thanks for your help!" Emma said, blowing them each a kiss. "I'll see you soon!" Then she vanished.

"At least one magic egg is safe," Rachel said.

55

"That's good," agreed Kirsty. "But now, we'd better get back to Mr. Hopper's and buy those eggs for my mom."

Back at the market, the girls found one carton of eggs that the goblins hadn't broken. They also found a crowd of happy—but confused!—customers.

"Look, my chocolate bunny isn't melted any more," said one man.

Another woman munched on some jelly beans. "And these are delicious!"

"It looks like all the Easter candies are yummy again," Kirsty said.

Rachel grinned. "Maybe we should try some, just to be sure."

That night, the girls nibbled on chocolate bunnies while they dyed Easter eggs. Mrs. Tate gave them six small cups. The girls put drops of dye in each cup and added some vinegar. Soon different bubbling bright colors filled the cups: pink, yellow, green, purple, blue, and orange.

"It's almost like fairy magic," Kirsty whispered as she dipped an egg into the yellow dye.

"I hope they turn out bright and beautiful," Rachel said, worried. "The magic egg that gives Easter eggs their extra sparkle is still missing."

"And so is the egg that helps the Easter Bunny," Kirsty added.

Kirsty gently put her yellow egg on a paper towel to dry. And as she did, the shell started to crack and break. Then Emma popped out of the egg and flew up with a giggle!

"I'm sorry I broke your egg," she said. "It's just such a fun way to get into your world."

"That's okay, we have a lot!" Kirsty
said. "We're dyeing them for the big
Easter egg hunt tomorrow at Daffodil
Field. Wetherbury holds one every year
on the day before Easter."

"That sounds like fun," Emma said. She
scratched her head and looked nervous.
"But we're so close to Easter, and we still
haven't found the Easter Bunny!"

"We still have a whole day to find
him," Rachel assured her.

"Yes, and you still have *us* to help you,"
Kirsty reminded her.

Emma brightened. "You're right!
If anyone can find the Easter Bunny,
we can!"

59

BOOK TWO

ROTTEN EGG HUNT
TABLE OF CONTENTS

A MAGICAL FEELING

"Are you sure it's okay if we head out early?" Kirsty's mom asked as she put on her coat. "We volunteered to help hide the eggs for the big Easter egg hunt, so we need to beat the crowd."

It was the morning before Easter. Rachel and Kirsty had stayed up past their bedtime, whispering about all the adventures they'd had the day before.

Now they were finishing the delicious blueberry pancakes Mrs. Tate had made for breakfast.

"It's fine, Mom," Kirsty said, smiling. "We'll meet you at Daffodil Field when the Easter egg hunt starts."

That will give us some time to figure out how we're going to find the other two missing eggs, Kirsty thought. *And the Easter Bunny, too!*

Outside, a car horn beeped. Mrs. Tate gave each of the girls a quick kiss.

"See you later! I bet you'll both find lots of eggs," she said before hurrying out the door.

Rachel yawned. "How many eggs do they hide for the egg hunt?" she asked Kirsty.

"It must be hundreds!" Kirsty replied, her eyes shining brightly with excitement. "The entire field is covered with blooming daffodils. The eggs are hidden all over the field."

"That sounds pretty," Rachel said dreamily. Just then, the air over the table shimmered for a moment.

"I love daffodils!" a voice called
out cheerfully. Emma appeared in the
air, fluttering her wings and grinning.
"They're always in bloom at Easter."

Rachel waved hello to their fairy friend.
"You should come to the egg hunt,"
she suggested.

Kirsty nodded.
"You would
love it. Besides,
an Easter egg
hunt would be
a perfect hiding
place for a
magic egg,
wouldn't it?"

Emma clapped
her hands
together.

"Oh, you're right!" she cried happily. "Can we go there now?"

Kirsty looked at the clock. "They don't let kids on the field until the eggs are hidden. But if we leave soon, we won't have to wait for long."

"Then let's go!" Emma said eagerly. "Tomorrow is Easter. Time is running out!"

The girls quickly cleaned up their breakfast dishes, changed out of their pajamas, and headed to Daffodil Field. Their walk took them through Wetherbury, past the town center.

Emma started to shiver as they passed the pet store. "There's that magical feeling again," she said, looking around. Mr. Hopper's market was right down the street. "I wonder what it could be."

67

"Yesterday we found the magic egg in the market after you shivered," Kirsty said. "Maybe there's another one there."

"We could check," Rachel suggested.

"Okay, but be on the lookout for Jack Frost's goblins," Emma warned. Then she darted out of sight into Kirsty's sweater pocket.

Things were much cleaner and quieter in the market that morning. There were no long lines of people making complaints. The jelly beans and broken eggs had all been cleaned up. But behind the counter, Mr. Hopper looked sad.

"Is everything okay, Mr. Hopper?" Kirsty asked.

Mr. Hopper had gray hair and a round face. He pushed his eyeglasses up on his nose when he saw Kirsty.

"Oh, it's nothing, dear. Tomorrow is Easter, after all, and that's a happy day," he said, trying to smile. "And my chocolate has stopped melting. But today, I found that all of the eggs in the refrigerator were rotten! I had to throw them away."

Rachel and Kirsty glanced at one another. They knew why the eggs were rotten!

Mr. Hopper pointed to the refrigerator, which was empty. "It's terrible not to have any eggs for Easter," he went on. "But I have a new shipment coming in this afternoon. I hope *those* eggs are all right."

"I'm sure they will be," Kirsty assured him.

Mr. Hopper patted her on the shoulder. "That's nice of you to say. Is there anything I can get for you?" he asked.

"Not right now," Kirsty replied. There were clearly no more magic eggs at Mr. Hopper's market. "We're going to Daffodil Field."

"Have fun, girls,"
Mr. Hopper said
with a smile.

As the girls
left the market,
Emma flew out of
Kirsty's pocket.

"This is terrible,"
Rachel said. "Those
eggs are going bad
because the magic egg
is missing. We have to find it so Mr.
Hopper has some eggs to sell!"

"That's exactly what I was thinking,"
Kirsty said. "Maybe we can find it at
Daffodil Field."

Emma fluttered between the girls.

"I didn't get that magical shiver in the
market. It's very strange."

71

"I'm sure we'll figure it out," Rachel assured her. With that, the girls continued their walk to Daffodil Field.

As they got closer, they could hear the sound of the excited crowd. Parents and kids waited along the edge of the field for the event to start. The kids clutched colorful Easter baskets.

Rachel gasped at the sight. Hundreds of daffodils were in bloom!

The yellow flowers were so bright they looked like the shining sun. The field was so big that Rachel couldn't even see where it ended.

"It's so pretty!" she cried.

"I'll have to paint a picture of this when I get home," Emma said, peeking out of Kirsty's pocket. "Everyone in Fairyland would love to see it!"

Kirsty's dad started speaking through a megaphone.

"The Easter egg hunt will begin when the whistle blows!" Mr. Tate announced.

"Please don't step on the daffodils as you search. There are plenty of eggs for everyone!"

"Oh, dear," Emma said, suddenly nervous. "There are so many kids here. What if one of them finds a magic egg before we do?"

"Don't worry," Rachel said. "I can run really fast."

"Me too," Kirsty added. "Besides, we know what we're looking for. I'm sure we'll spot one of the magic eggs, if it's here."

The girls walked to the starting line and each grabbed a basket.

Tweeeeet! Mr. Tate blew his whistle.

"Let the Easter egg hunt begin!" he cried.

DAFFODIL DISGUISES

Rachel and Kirsty raced between the rows of daffodils. They spotted lots of eggs as they ran. Strangely, the eggs weren't bright colors—yellow, green, blue, purple, pink, or orange. The colors were faded, and some were even brown or gray.

"Yuck!" Rachel exclaimed, stopping to look at an egg.

"We need to find the magic egg that helps make all Easter eggs bright and beautiful," Emma reminded the girls quietly. "Without that egg's magic, the Easter eggs won't look pretty."

Kirsty stopped and scanned the field of daffodils.

"We're looking for an egg that's white, with a picture painted on it," she said. "That should stick out in this yellow and green field."

Rachel pointed to an area up ahead. "Maybe it's by those big daffodils over there," she suggested.

The girls hurried toward the big daffodils, and Emma fluttered along beside them. They were a few rows away when Emma suddenly stopped in midair.

"Wait," she warned. "I don't think those are daffodils. Look!"

The daffodils were moving! Not only that, they were talking, too!

"There are so many eggs here! How are we supposed to find a magic egg?" one of the daffodils grumbled.

"Just keep looking," another daffodil said crossly. "Jack Frost will be so angry if we don't find one."

"They're goblins!" Rachel realized.

"We'd better duck," Kirsty whispered, crouching down.

The girls got a closer look at the goblins in disguise. Each goblin wore a hat on their heads that looked like a yellow daffodil. Their green bodies and clothes looked like flower stems. And they had fake green leaves strapped to each arm. There were at least five goblins dressed as daffodils!

The goblins started to become loud and rowdy as they searched for the egg.

"It's over there!" one yelled.

"No, it's over there!" another one shouted.

The goblins tripped over each other as they scrambled to find the magic egg.

"*Ow*! You're stepping on my petals!" a goblin whined.

"We'd better get moving," Rachel said. "We can't let those goblins beat us to the egg this time!" The girls started looking through the daffodils once more. They hadn't gotten far when they heard the sound of a child crying. "Oh, no!" Emma cried. "Someone is in trouble."

81

A STINKY PROBLEM

The girls hurried toward the sound of
the crying child. They found two little
girls and a boy standing around a pile
of broken eggs. Luckily, there were no
goblins around. But something still
wasn't right.

Rachel wrinkled her nose. "Those
eggs are smelly!"

Kirsty nodded. "They look rotten."

One of the little girls was crying. "These Easter eggs aren't nice. I want my mommy!"

Rachel and Kirsty heard the sound of the goblins getting closer.

"Something smells nice and stinky!" one of the goblins said.

"Just like Mom's cooking! Yum!" agreed another goblin.

Emma peeked out from her hiding place inside Kirsty's pocket.

"We have to get these kids away, quickly!" she warned. "Otherwise, they might see the goblins."

Kirsty thought fast and turned back to the children. "We saw some pretty eggs over there," she said, pointing far away from the goblins.

A Stinky Problem

The sad little girl wiped the tears from her cheeks. "Really?"

Kirsty nodded. "Why don't you go and look for them?"

The kids' faces brightened and they scampered away.

Rachel frowned. "Kirsty, that was a lie!"

"I know," Kirsty replied. "I don't like lying. But we have to get them away from the goblins, and that was the only thing I could think of to do."

"Well, now we have to find the magic egg *fast!*" Rachel said. "If we don't, the whole Easter egg hunt will be ruined."

Emma flew out of Kirsty's pocket. "I'll have a better view if I fly over the field," she said.

"But then everyone might see you," Kirsty reminded her.

Emma thought for a moment, then grinned. "I have an idea."

She waved her wand in a circle. Rainbow-colored sparkles appeared like tiny fireworks in the air. Then she called out in a singsong voice:
"Help me please, my butterfly friends. The goblins are up to their evil ends."

86

Rachel and Kirsty watched, amazed, as the air around them filled with beautiful butterflies! Their wings shimmered in the sunlight. Some were blue, some were yellow, and some were orange.

Emma laughed and flew up into the middle of the crowd of butterflies. She fluttered her delicate wings. "See? If anyone spots me, they'll think I'm a butterfly!"

"Great idea!" Rachel said. "We'll keep looking down here while you search from the sky."

Emma and the butterflies flew off across the field.

"Finally, that pesky fairy is gone!" a voice cried out.

The girls froze. The daffodils around them jumped up. But they weren't daffodils at all. Rachel and Kirsty were surrounded by goblins!

"Ha! Our plan worked!" a goblin cried, gesturing to his friends. "We'll stay and keep these girls out of the way. The other goblins will follow that fairy to the magic egg!"

The group of goblins laughed.

Rachel and Kirsty were a little bit afraid— but only a little bit. They had outsmarted Jack Frost's goblins before.

"What should we do?" Kirsty whispered to Rachel.

"Run past them?" Rachel suggested.

"Maybe, but there are a lot of them," Kirsty replied. "They might catch us."

"Hey! No talking!" a goblin snapped.

Kirsty smiled sweetly. "Sorry. We were just saying how pretty you all look!"

The goblins frowned.

"Pretty? We're not pretty! We're goblins!" one of them protested. "But you look like pretty flowers," Kirsty said.

The goblins grumbled. Rachel smiled at Kirsty. She knew what her friend was trying to do.

"Well, not *all* of you are pretty," Rachel said. She pointed to one of the goblins. "You look scary. In fact, *you* might be the scariest one."

The goblin looked proud. "Of course! I'm the scariest of all!"

The other goblins didn't like that.

"No, *I'm* the scariest!"

"No, it's me!"

"Nobody is scarier than I am!"

The goblins started to argue. Soon they were shoving and wrestling each other, just like they had done in the market.

Rachel nudged Kirsty. "They're distracted. Let's run!"

EGG-CITEMENT!

Rachel and Kirsty ran straight past the fighting goblins. The goblins were so busy arguing, they didn't even notice!

"Now we have to find Emma before the other goblins do," Rachel said.

The girls scanned the field. A few rows away, they saw the butterflies hovering over a small daffodil patch.

"Over there!" Kirsty cried.

The girls ran toward the butterflies. They spotted a small group of goblins running from the other direction.

Kirsty tried to run faster. "They're going to beat us there!"

"Maybe we can stop them," Rachel said.

"How?" Kirsty asked.

Rachel quickly bent down and scooped up an Easter egg from under a daffodil leaf. It looked gray and smelled bad.

Kirsty did the same. Their baskets were filled with rotten eggs by the time they reached Emma.

Emma turned her head and waved when she saw them.

"I found it!" the fairy called out. "One of the magic eggs!"

The girls saw a white egg perched in the center of a daffodil. It had a picture of a colorful Easter egg painted on it and it sparkled with fairy magic.

But two of the goblins had already reached Emma.

"I'll take that!" one of them said, grabbing for the egg.

Rachel nodded at Kirsty. "Now!"

The girls pelted the two goblins with rotten eggs. The eggs broke as they hit the goblins, splattering them with smelly goo.

"Oh, no!" one of them yelled.

"Yuck!" shouted the other. "It's slimy and cold. This is even worse than having cold, wet feet!"

They ran off, leaving the magic egg inside the flower.

Kirsty hurried to the daffodil and picked up the egg. Emma fluttered down next to her, smiling widely.

"Good work, girls!" she cheered. "You did a great job getting rid of those goblins." Emma turned to the butterflies. "Thank you for your help!"

The butterflies flew away across the field

in a blur of beautiful colors.

Kirsty looked down at the egg in her hand. "This is the magic egg that makes Easter eggs bright and beautiful, isn't it?"

Emma nodded. "Yes! I should get it back to Fairyland quickly, before any more goblins show up to cause trouble."

The fairy waved her wand over the magic egg. The egg shrank down to its fairy-size. Then it floated up and landed in Emma's palm.

"I'll be back soon," Emma told the girls. "We still have one more magic egg to find."

"And the Easter Bunny, too," Rachel added.

Emma nodded, blowing each girl a kiss. She flapped her wings, and the air around her sparkled and shimmered. Then she vanished.

RAINBOW MAGIC

Just then, the three kids they'd seen earlier came running back to Rachel and Kirsty. They looked angry.

"There you are," said the little girl who had been crying. "You told us there were nice eggs over there. But we didn't find any! Just these!"

She held out her Easter basket. It was filled with gray and brown eggs.

"They're all yucky!" complained the little boy next to her. He crossed his arms in front of him.

At that moment, a beautiful rainbow appeared over the field. Everyone began to *ooh* and *ahh* as they peered up at the sky. The rainbow colors sparkled over the whole field of daffodils.

"Do you think it's fairy magic?" Rachel whispered.

"I think so," Kirsty said, gazing around the field. "Look!"

The gray and brown eggs in the field were changing color right before their eyes! Now they were bright pink, yellow, and blue, with colorful polka dots and swirly designs.

"Your eggs look very nice to me," Kirsty told the little girl.

The three children looked inside the Easter basket and gasped.

"They're so pretty!" the girl cried.

The little boy's eyes were wide when he looked back up at Kirsty. "You must be magic!"

Kirsty grinned. "It's the magic of Easter," she said.

"There are pretty eggs all over the field now," Rachel told them. "You should go and find more."

"Hooray!" the children cheered, running off.

"We should get some eggs, too," Kirsty said, turning back to Rachel. "Our parents will wonder why we don't have any if we come back empty-handed."

Rachel looked worried. "I hope there are some left for us!"

The girls raced through the field once again. Now that they didn't have to worry about goblins, it was fun looking for the Easter eggs.

Rachel found a purple one with yellow stars tucked under a daffodil. Kirsty found an orange egg with blue flowers all over it. Each egg they found was nicer than the last.

"Emma's Easter magic is amazing!" Rachel said. "These are the most beautiful eggs I've ever seen."

"Me, too!" Kirsty agreed.

When there were no more eggs in the field, the girls met up with their parents.

"There you are," said Kirsty's mom. "How did you do?"

Kirsty held up her basket. "We found lots of nice eggs!"

Rachel's mom joined them. "Are you sure?" she asked. "Some of the kids were complaining that their eggs were rotten."

Mrs. Tate looked around. "That's funny. All of the eggs look fine to me."

Rachel and Kirsty smiled at each other. The magic egg was doing its work! All of the Easter eggs were bright and beautiful again.

"What do you say we head home for some lunch?" Mrs. Tate asked. "I'll make some egg salad."

"Yum!" the girls said at the same time.

They rode home in the Tates' car, past the stores in Wetherbury. Through the market window, Rachel and Kirsty could see Mr. Hopper selling a carton of eggs to a customer. The store owner had a happy smile on his face.

"It looks like Mr. Hopper's shipment of eggs came in," Kirsty remarked.

"Just in time!" Rachel added.

Then they passed the pet store. The sign on the door read OPEN.

"I thought the pet store was closed for Easter," Kirsty said.

"I thought so, too," said Mrs. Tate from the front seat. "Mrs. Gilligan went to stay with her daughter, who lives by the beach. Perhaps she got somebody to watch the store for her."

That seemed a little strange to Kirsty. She thought about it for the rest of the car ride. She brought it up when she and Rachel were eating their egg salad sandwiches at the picnic table outside.

"I've been thinking about the pet store," Kirsty began.

Rachel nodded her head eagerly. "Me too!" she said. "Emma got that magical feeling every time we passed it."

"And it's strange that it was closed for Easter, but now it's open," Kirsty added.

"Strange or *magical*?" Rachel asked, taking a bite of her sandwich.

"Good question," Kirsty said thoughtfully.

"We should go back to the pet store after lunch," Rachel suggested.

"That's a good idea," Kirsty agreed. "But I think my parents have more Easter plans for us."

"We have to find a way," Rachel said, lowering her voice. "If we don't track down the last missing egg and the Easter Bunny, everyone's Easter plans will be ruined!"

BOOK THREE

THE EASTER BUNNY INCIDENT
TABLE OF CONTENTS

109

A TRAP

"Mom, what are we doing this afternoon?" Kirsty asked after lunch.

Mrs. Tate smiled. "Mr. and Mrs. Harrison are inviting people to visit Strawberry Farm today," she said. "There were lots of animals born this spring, and we'll be able to meet them."

"Oh, baby animals are so cute!" Rachel exclaimed, grinning. "Will there be lambs?"

Kirsty's mom nodded. "And goats, and calves, and baby ducks, too."

Going to the farm sounded like a lot of fun. But Kirsty and Rachel were worried. They had to find the last missing magic egg *and* the Easter Bunny by the end of the day. If they didn't, Easter wouldn't be the same!

"Do Rachel and I have time to go for a walk first?" Kirsty asked.

Mrs. Tate looked at the kitchen clock.

"We're leaving for the farm at two o'clock, so you have a little bit of time. Go out and enjoy the beautiful day!"

Kirsty nodded to Rachel, and the girls stepped outside into the bright sunshine.

"Now we'll have time to check out the pet store," Kirsty said.

"I have a good feeling that we'll find something important there," Rachel added. "There must be a reason why Emma got a magical feeling every time we walked past that place."

Kirsty looked around. "Emma? Are you here?"

The Easter Fairy appeared in a sparkly spray of fairy dust. "King Oberon and Queen Titania were so happy that we found the second magic egg!" she cried, twirling through the air. "They told me to thank you both."

"We're glad to help," Kirsty said, smiling at her fairy friend. "And we have an idea. We're going back to the pet store in town. We think something strange is happening there."

"I'll come with you," Emma told them, suddenly looking serious.

Emma flew into Kirsty's pocket and the friends hurried to the pet store together. As they turned the corner onto Main Street, Emma suddenly spoke up.

"Look! Up there! It's an egg!"

Emma pointed to a crook in the branch of a tree right next to the pet store. The girls could see something sparkly and white there.

Emma was quivering with excitement. "I'll fly up and get it!"

She darted out of Kirsty's pocket, heading straight for the egg. But before she reached it, Emma stopped in midair.

"Oh, no!" she cried.

"Emma, what's wrong?" Kirsty asked.

"I'm stuck!" the little fairy said in dismay. "It's Goblin Gossamer! Their pet spiders weave it. It's very, very sticky. I can't move my wings!"

Rachel shaded her eyes with her hand so she could see better. She spotted Emma up above, struggling, but she couldn't see anything else around the fairy. "I can't see anything," she said, squinting.

"Goblin Gossamer is invisible," Emma told them. "Goblins like to use it to trap fairies. The only way to get out is to sprinkle it with fairy dust."

"Can you use your wand?" Kirsty asked, worried.

"No!" Emma called down. "I can't move my arms."

Rachel's eyes got wide. How could they possibly help Emma now? Then she looked at the locket hanging around Kirsty's neck. Rachel had a matching one of her own. They were presents from the king and queen of the fairies . . . and they were filled with magical fairy dust!

"It's a good thing we have some fairy dust," Rachel said.

She opened up her locket and sprinkled some of the fairy dust onto her palm.

Kirsty did the same. Then the two girls blew gently on the fairy dust. It floated into the air, leaving a trail of sparkles behind it.

When the fairy dust swirled around Emma, the invisible Goblin Gossamer became visible. It looked like a green spider web.

After a moment, the strands of the web dissolved, and Emma was free!

"Oh, thank you," Emma cried in relief, flying down to the girls. "I could have been trapped there for a long time, if it wasn't for you!"

"The goblins must have set that trap," Rachel guessed. "They were trying to keep you from getting the magic egg back!"

Emma shook her head. "No, that wasn't the magic egg at all. It was a plastic egg sprinkled with glitter."

"Then why set a trap?" Rachel wondered. She scratched her head.

Kirsty frowned. "I think they're trying to keep us away from the pet store."

Just then, the big town clock began to chime. It was two o'clock!

"Oh, no!" Kirsty cried. "We have to get home fast. We're late!"

SO CUTE!

Kirsty and Rachel ran back to Kirsty's house as quickly as they could.

"Meet us at Strawberry Farm," Kirsty told Emma as they got close.

Emma flew out of Kirsty's pocket. "See you later!" she called, then vanished in a twinkle of light.

Mrs. Tate and Mrs. Walker were waiting for the girls in the driveway.

"There you are," Kirsty's mom said, opening the car door. "Your dads are going to stay at home and start getting dinner ready. We'll take you to the farm."

Kirsty and Rachel climbed into the back seat of the Tates' car.

"I can't wait to see the baby animals," Rachel said eagerly. "We don't have any farms like that in Tippington."

"But your town has lots of other fun things to do," Kirsty pointed out. "I loved picnicking at Windy Lake."

When they arrived at the farm, the gravel parking lot was filled with cars. The porch of the big white farmhouse was decorated with dangling paper Easter eggs. Next to the house stood a red barn with some animals inside. Visitors were walking around a fenced-in field next to the barn. The air smelled of sweet, fresh hay.

THE EASTER BUNNY INCIDENT

Rachel bolted out of the car and ran to see the baby animals.

"Hey, wait up!" Kirsty called out.

Rachel paused at the fence. "Aww, they're *so* cute!"

In the pen in front of her were three small lambs with curly white wool. Next to them were two brown-and-white calves with big, brown eyes. Gray baby goats munched on hay in another pen.

And in the last pen, fuzzy yellow baby ducks splashed in a small pond.

"They *are* awfully cute," Kirsty agreed.

Rachel reached through the fence to pet one of the lambs. "Hi there, little guy," she said.

Cock-a-doodle-doo!

A loud crow of a rooster rang across the farm.

Rachel jumped. "What was that?" she asked, looking around.

"It's a rooster," Kirsty replied.

"Do they have chickens here?" Rachel asked.

Kirsty nodded. "There's a big coop behind the barn."

Rachel looked thoughtful. After a moment, her eyes lit up. "Kirsty! Where there are chickens . . ."

". . . there are eggs!" Kirsty said, finishing her thought.

The girls looked at each other meaningfully.

"Do you think the last missing magic egg could be in the chicken coop?" Rachel whispered.

Kirsty grinned, her eyes shining. "I think it's a good place to look!"

Together, they walked around the big red barn. Through the open door, they saw some big cows and lots of sheep munching on hay.

"Those must be the mommy and daddy animals," Rachel said.

Kirsty looked around. "I wonder where Emma is?"

They turned the corner of the barn, and found themselves face-to-face with a small group of lambs.

"What are you doing out of your pen?" Rachel said. "Are you lost?"

"No," replied one of the lambs. "But we want *you* to get lost!"

Rachel and Kirsty gasped and stepped back. These weren't baby sheep at all.

They were goblins!

DANCING CHICKENS

The goblins were wearing fuzzy lamb costumes, but their green heads stuck out from under the fake lamb heads.

Rachel put her hands on her hips. "Get out of our way!" she said bravely.

But the goblins stood in a straight line in front of them, blocking their path.

"No way!" one of the goblins said.

"We're under strict orders from Jack Frost. You girls keep messing everything up!"

"*You're* the ones messing everything up!" Kirsty shot back. "Why can't you just go away and let everyone have a nice Easter?"

The goblins didn't answer. Instead, their eyes grew wide. They looked afraid.

Kirsty and Rachel turned to see Emma flying toward them! Glittering fairy dust

flew from her wand. All the big cows
and sheep were following the fairy dust!
When they saw the disguised goblins,
their eyes got angry.

"*Moo*!" bellowed the cows.

"*Baaaa*!" cried the sheep.

The animals charged past Kirsty
and Rachel and stomped toward the
goblins.

"Run!" one of the goblins cried.

The goblins scrambled
in all directions,
leaving their lamb
costumes behind.

Emma flew up
to the cows and
sheep. "Thank
you, my friends,"
she said kindly.

"*Mooo*," replied one
of the cows, nodding.

The animals slowly returned to the
barn, while Emma fluttered over to
Rachel and Kirsty.

"You got here just in time!" Kirsty
said gratefully.

"Yes," Rachel added, nodding.
"Thank you!"

"Those goblins are *such* a pain!"

Emma replied, frowning. "I hope we've got rid of them for a while."

"Me too," said Kirsty. They had important things to do! "Rachel and I were just going to the chicken coop to look for the missing egg."

Emma fluttered her wings happily. "Oh, what a wonderful idea! Let's go!"

The chicken coop was a large wooden building with wide shelves built along one side. The shelves held rows of small nesting boxes filled with hay, so the chickens could lay their eggs there. Almost every box had a fat, white chicken sitting on it.

"Where are the eggs?" Rachel asked, looking around.

"Underneath the chickens," Kirsty explained. "They sit on the eggs after they lay them. I've helped Mr. and Mrs. Harrison collect the eggs before. But the chickens don't always like it. Sometimes they make a fuss."

"Then it won't be easy to look for the magic egg, will it?" Rachel asked.

"I know a way," Emma said brightly. "Back home, my pet chicken, Fluffy, loves to dance. This is her favorite song."

Emma began to sing in her musical fairy voice. *"Cluck, cluck, cluck! Cluck, cluck, cluck!"*

Emma's voice carried through the coop. The happy chickens stood up one by one, hopping from one foot to the other.

"That's amazing!" Rachel said, her eyes wide in wonder.

Kirsty ran to the nesting boxes and looked under one of the chickens. "If there's a magic egg here, we'll find it."

"Wonderful!" Emma exclaimed. "You girls can sing with me, too, if you want."

"*Cluck, cluck, cluck! Cluck, cluck, cluck!*"

Rachel and Kirsty joined in. Now all the chickens were standing up. Some moved their heads back and forth to the music.

The girls raced along the rows of boxes, hoping to spot the magic egg. At first, they just saw one plain white egg after another. But then they both noticed something at the same time.

The biggest chicken in the coop was standing over a beautiful, sparkly egg! As the girls got closer, they could see that it had a picture of an Easter basket painted on it.

Kirsty gingerly reached underneath the chicken and grabbed the egg. It glittered with fairy magic in her hand.

"We did it!" Kirsty cried. "We found the last magic egg!"

A PET STORE SURPRISE

"Oh, this is amazing!" Emma cried happily. She flew to Kirsty and waved her wand over the magic egg. It shrunk down to fairy-size, and Emma scooped it up. "Once I return this to Fairyland, the Easter Bunny will have the magic he needs to deliver baskets to boys and girls everywhere."

Kirsty frowned. "But we still have to find the Easter Bunny," she reminded Emma.

Emma nodded. "I know. But I'm very hopeful. Thanks to you girls, we've found the three magic eggs. Somehow, I just know we'll find the Easter Bunny."

"We'll do our best," Rachel said.

"I need to take this egg to Fairyland," Emma told them. "But I'll come back and find you as soon as I can."

"And we'll keep looking for the Easter Bunny," Kirsty promised.

Emma waved to them as she vanished in a swirl of twinkling light. By now, the chickens were all sitting on their nests again.

"We should try to go back to the pet store," Kirsty suggested. "I just have a feeling about that place."

"Right," Rachel agreed. "Only this time, we need to keep an eye out for goblin traps!"

The girls walked back to the pens where the baby animals were kept. Mrs. Walker and Mrs. Tate were feeding corn to the baby goats.

"That tickles!" Rachel's mom said with a laugh. She looked up when she saw the girls. "Are you having fun?"

"Definitely!" Rachel said. "Mom, can we get a baby lamb at our house?"

"I don't think we have room in our backyard!" Mrs. Walker replied.

"But you can always visit us and come back to Strawberry Farm whenever you like," Mrs. Tate said.

Mrs. Walker brushed the corn crumbs off her hands. "We should wash up before we head home."

"I need to stop at the market on the way back," said Mrs. Tate.

That gave Kirsty an idea. "Can I show Rachel the pet store while you're shopping?"

"I don't see why not," her mom replied. "It's just a few doors down."

Kirsty and Rachel looked at each other. They were both thinking the same thing: maybe they would finally find out what was happening in the pet store!

When they got to town, Kirsty and Rachel waved to their moms and cautiously walked up to the pet store. They saw a sparkly egg sitting on top of a mailbox nearby.

"Another trap!" Kirsty said. "But it won't work this time. We've already found all the missing eggs."

A bell tinkled as they pushed open the door of the pet store. Half of the store was filled with shelves stocked with pet food, toys, and bowls. The other half was filled with tanks and cages of small pets—hamsters, rabbits, and snakes.

A few customers were looking at the
animals, while others shopped for supplies.

Kirsty and Rachel walked through
the aisles, looking around.

"Everything seems normal," Rachel
remarked. She shrugged.

"I know," Kirsty said. "I wish Emma
was here. She could tell us if she felt
something magical."

Suddenly, Rachel stopped. "Kirsty, look
over there!"

Rachel pointed to the big pen in the corner that had been set up for rabbits. It held a small, brown rabbit, a black-and-white rabbit with floppy ears, and a fluffy white rabbit.

The white rabbit was sparkling with fairy magic!

"Do you think it could be the Easter Bunny?" Kirsty whispered.

"May I help you, girls?" asked a voice behind them.

The girls spun around and gasped. They knew that voice!

"Jack Frost! What are you doing here?" Rachel asked bravely.

Jack Frost grinned. He was taller than the goblins, with spiky white hair, and a pointy nose and ears.

"I'm sorry, my name is Mr. Jackson," he said. "I'm a friend of Mrs. Gilligan's. She asked me to watch the store while she's away."

"You can't fool us!" Kirsty said, crossing her arms. "We know what you're doing. You've kidnapped the Easter Bunny!"

Jack Frost chuckled coldly. "What lively imaginations you have. Now, if you don't mind, I must ask you to leave the store. You're disturbing the customers."

"But we're not—" Rachel began, but Kirsty stopped her.

"Come on, Rachel," she said.

Rachel and Kirsty left the store.

"Why did we leave?" Rachel asked, confused. "I think that white bunny in the pen might be the Easter Bunny!"

"I do, too," Kirsty said. "But Jack Frost isn't like an ordinary goblin. He has very powerful magic. We can't beat him without Emma's help!"

HAPPY EASTER!

"Here I am!" Emma cried just then, popping into the air in front of them. "The last magic egg is safe in Fairyland."

"Jack Frost is inside the pet store!" Kirsty told her immediately.

"And we think we found the Easter Bunny," Rachel added. "But we're not sure. It looks like a regular white rabbit, but it's all sparkly, like it might be magical."

"Oh, that's fabulous news! Jack Frost must be using a spell to make the Easter Bunny look like an ordinary rabbit. That's not his true form, of course. We must get him back right away!"

"But Jack Frost is guarding the shop," Kirsty pointed out. "How will we get past him?"

Emma was thoughtful. "We need a distraction of some kind. Then I can fly in, wave my wand over the Easter Bunny, and send him home."

Just then, a group of grumbling goblins approached on the empty sidewalk. The goblins looked dirty, and some of them had fake wool from their lamb costumes stuck to their green skin.

"Jack Frost is going to be mad!" said one goblin.

"We didn't find the magic egg!" wailed another.

"It wasn't our fault! It was those scary cows and sheep," complained another.

Emma grinned. "Goblins always make a good distraction!" she said brightly. Then she whispered her idea to the girls. "Do you think you can do it?"

Kirsty nodded. "Just watch." She turned to Rachel. "I'm so excited!" she said in a loud voice.

"Me too!" shouted Rachel. "The last magic egg is inside the pet store."

"But it's in the snake tank," Kirsty replied loudly, biting her lip. "I'm too scared to reach into the tank to get it!"

The goblins raced up to them.

"We're not scared!" one of them bragged.

"We're going to get that magic egg before you do!" taunted another.

The goblins ran into the pet store with

the girls and Emma following close
behind. They peeked around a shelf and
watched as the goblins pulled open the
lid of the snake tank. Then they started
picking up the snakes and waving them in
the air.

"Where is it? Where is the magic egg?"
they cried.

The snakes slid out of their hands and
started crawling on the floor.

155

Jack Frost came around the corner—and he was furious. "What are you doing?" he screamed at his goblins. "Put those snakes down!"

Emma winked at Rachel and Kirsty, and flew to the rabbit pen. Jack Frost was so busy yelling that he didn't even see her.

The girls watched as Emma waved her magic wand over the Easter Bunny three times. A cloud of glittering fairy dust surrounded the rabbit. The cloud lifted the white bunny up, up, up into the air.

That's when Jack Frost finally noticed. "No!" he yelled. He ran toward the rabbit pen.

But he was too late.

Poof! The Easter Bunny disappeared.

"That's not fair!" Jack Frost cried, swatting at Emma. But she only giggled before vanishing too.

"Jack Frost looks really angry," Rachel remarked.

"We'd better get out of here," Kirsty whispered, edging quietly toward the door.

The girls ran back to the market as quickly as they could.

Back home, Rachel and Kirsty helped get dinner ready. Afterward, they played board games with their parents. There was no sign of Emma anywhere!

Later, Kirsty and Rachel snuggled into their beds. They hadn't been able to talk about what had happened that day until bedtime, in case their parents overheard.

"I wonder where Emma is," Kirsty said.

"It's the night before Easter," Rachel reminded her. "I'm sure she's very busy."

Kirsty yawned. "I guess so. I just hope she got back to Fairyland okay."

"I know she did," Rachel said. "We saw her. And all three magic eggs are safely back, too."

"That's right," Kirsty agreed. "That means that Easter candy will taste delicious, Easter eggs will be bright and beautiful, and the Easter Bunny will deliver baskets to boys and girls all over the world."

Kirsty's door opened, and Kirsty's mom peeked inside.

"Go to sleep, girls," she said. "The Easter Bunny is coming tonight!"

"We know, Mom," Kirsty said, winking at Rachel.

The girls drifted off into a deep sleep. In the morning, they both woke up at the same time. Bright sunlight shone through the window. Outside, the spring birds were singing a happy song.

"The Easter Bunny!" Kirsty and Rachel cried.

They scrambled out of bed and ran downstairs. On the kitchen table were two beautiful Easter baskets. A tag on one read KIRSTY, and the other read RACHEL.

"He came!" Rachel said.

The girls' parents came into the kitchen, yawning.

"I see the Easter Bunny visited last night," Rachel's dad said with a grin.

Kirsty grabbed her basket. "Come on!" she told Rachel. "Let's see what he brought."

The girls took their baskets onto the sunny porch and sat on the steps. They looked through the shiny Easter grass.

Kirsty found a chocolate egg and popped it into her mouth. "Yum!"

Rachel ate a red jelly bean. "It tastes like strawberries!"

"And look," Kirsty said, picking up a dyed Easter egg with purple and pink swirls. "It's bright and beautiful!"

THE EASTER BUNNY INCIDENT

Then Kirsty saw the grass in her Easter basket start to move. Out flew the best Easter gift of all—Emma!

"Happy Easter!" she cried, hovering in front of the girls.

"Happy Easter, Emma!" the girls said together, grinning.

"King Oberon and Queen Titania are so happy that you helped us find the Easter Bunny," Emma said. "They sent you each a special gift. Go ahead, look inside your baskets."

The girls eagerly dug through the brightly colored Easter grass. At the same time, they each pulled out a beautiful golden egg.

"Open them up!" Emma told them.

Each egg had a hinge on the back, and they opened right in the middle. A beautiful tune began to play, and inside, a tiny fairy in a yellow dress twirled around and around.

"Emma, that's you!" Kirsty realized.

Emma clapped her hands, delighted.

"Aren't they wonderful?"

"She looks just like you," Rachel said.

"Please make sure to thank the king and queen for us."

"Of course!" Emma said. She twirled around in the air in front of them.

"Well, I have to head off now. Today is a busy day! But thanks again, girls. Have a happy Easter."

Rachel and Kirsty smiled at each other.

"We definitely will!"

THE EASTER BUNNY INCIDENT

J E L L Y B E A N

Did you find all nine letters hidden throughout the book? The special Easter treat is **Jelly Bean**!

Now it's time for Kirsty and
Rachel to help . . .

TRIXIE THE HALLOWEEN FAIRY.

Read on for a sneak peek . . .

TRIXIE
THE HALLOWEEN FAIRY

BUTTONS BARKS

"I can't wait to show you the fairy wings," Rachel Walker said to her best friend, Kirsty Tate, as they climbed the stairs to Rachel's room.

"I'm excited to see them," Kirsty replied. "It will be so much fun to trick-or-treat together!"

Kirsty was visiting Rachel for the weekend, and it just happened to be Halloween! They were both going to dress up as fairies.

The two girls exchanged smiles as Rachel lifted the lid of a storage box. Inside were two sets of glittery fairy wings: one was pale pink and the other in a light purple.

"Oh, Rachel! They look almost real," Kirsty said, giving her friend a knowing look. After all, the girls knew just how real fairies' wings looked. They were friends with the fairies!

Rachel and Kirsty met during vacation with their families on beautiful Rainspell Island. There, they had helped the Rainbow Fairies get back to Fairyland after they had been banished by wicked Jack Frost. Since then, the girls had helped lots of fairies. Now the king and queen of Fairyland looked to them whenever Jack Frost was up to his old tricks.

"I'm going to try mine on," Kirsty said, carefully lifting up a sparkly set of wings.

Just then, they heard a loud bark. Buttons, Rachel's adorable sheepdog, raced into the room. He knocked into Kirsty and tore through the storage bin on his way to the window.

"Buttons!" Rachel yelled as the costumes flew up in the air. But Buttons kept barking at something outside. Then he turned to Rachel and whimpered. "What is it, boy?" Rachel asked with concern.

"Oh! There's a kitten in the tree!" Kirsty said, pointing out the window. The kitten was black from its nose to its tail.

"That's strange," Rachel said. "Buttons usually loves cats."

Now the big sheepdog pawed at the window.

"Do you think the kitten's stuck?" Kirsty asked. "Maybe it needs our help."

But at that moment, the little black cat leaped onto a nearby branch. It strutted past the window and seemed to look right at Buttons and the girls, then scurried down another tree.

173

RAINBOW magic

More Titles to Read

RAINBOW FAIRIES:
RUBY THE
RED FAIRY

RAINBOW FAIRIES:
AMBER THE
ORANGE FAIRY

RAINBOW FAIRIES:
SUNNY THE
YELLOW FAIRY

RAINBOW FAIRIES:
FERN THE
GREEN FAIRY

RAINBOW FAIRIES:
SKY THE
BLUE FAIRY

RAINBOW FAIRIES:
INKY THE
INDIGO FAIRY

RAINBOW FAIRIES:
HEATHER THE
VIOLET FAIRY

SPECIAL EDITION:
HOLLY THE
CHRISTMAS FAIRY

SPECIAL EDITION:
TRIXIE THE
HALLOWEEN FAIRY

☆ ☆ ☆ ☆ ☆ ☆ ☆

BEHIND THE MAGIC

DAISY MEADOWS is a pseudonym for the four writers of the internationally best-selling *Rainbow Magic* series: Narinder Dhami, Sue Bentley, Linda Chapman, and Sue Mongredien. *Rainbow Magic* is the no.1 bestselling series for children ages 5 and up with over 40 million copies sold worldwide!

GEORGIE RIPPER was born in London and is a children's book illustrator known for her work on the *Rainbow Magic* series of fairy books. She won the Macmillan Prize for Picture Book Illustration in 2000 with *My Best Friend Bob* and *Little Brown Bushrat*, which she wrote and illustrated.